Sigrid Heuck

Pony,
Bear and Snowstorm

Aus dem Deutschen von Hilary Schmitt-Thomas

Thienemann

The  and the were good friends.

Every year in autumn, when the

fell from the , the went to visit

the in the in the middle of

the .

Then they ate the from the that

was behind the the lived in.

And there was nothing in the world that tasted

better.

When they had eaten all the  ,

they spent a little time chatting.

But after a while, the  growled, "I've got to

go now. Winter will be here soon. Goodbye!"

This made the sad because it would be all

alone.

And so one day it said, "I'm coming with you."

"That's a good idea," growled the  .

And he set off and the 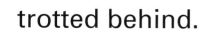 trotted behind.

On the day, they left the  and

the  . They went over a

across a  .

The wind blew the last

from the .

On the  day, they marched

over the and went past a  .

It got so cold that the ground froze.

On the  day, they came to the

and reached the 's  .

And the  fell from the sky.

At first, the  was afraid because it was

so dark in the . But then the

lit a . He made a and a of tea.

He fetched some for the ,

and a of water from a .

"We've got enough food and we've also got enough

water," he growled.

"And we've got each other," neighed the

happily.

Outside, a  of ❄️ covered

the 🌱 and the 🌲 , ⛰️

and 🏔️ .

So the 🧸 fetched his 🛷 , harnessed

the 🐴 to it and sat on it to be pulled along.

And when the 🐴 was tired, the 🧸 pulled

the 🛷 , and the 🐴 was the driver.

Later they started a snow 🔴 fight.

When it was dark, the  growled, "Goodnight!"

Then he lay down in his little  and covered

himself up.

"Sleep well!" neighed the  quietly and

made itself comfortable on a 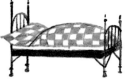 of  .

By the time the  in the  had said

"Tu-whit-tu-whoo", they were fast asleep.

It became bitterly cold.

A  storm raged over the .

The and the ,

the and the

hid away in their .

Only the had to stay outside.

The asked, "Aren't we lucky?"

And the neighed happily,

"Yes, you're right."

"I wonder what the 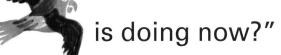 is doing now?"

the  said later. The  was an old friend.

"It's probably flying around in the rain

and annoying the 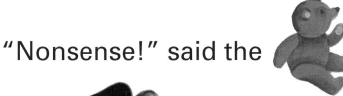," replied

the .

"Perhaps it's missing us," said the .

"Nonsense!" said the . "Last night, I dreamt

of the . It was hanging upside down from

a  with its ● 🦶🦶 and squawking with

pleasure."

"But it hasn't got ," said the .

"Its  are ●."

"No, ● !" said the . "I'm sure!"

"No, ● ."

"No, ● ."

"No, ● ."

And because the  and the couldn't

agree, they stopped speaking to each other.

The  said nothing,

and the didn't say anything, either.

They turned their backs on each other

and were cross.

They went to bed without saying goodnight.

And they were suddenly very cold.

The next morning, the  made a very good

 , but it was no use. It was still cold.

Even the  stood so close to the

that its was almost burnt. It shivered with cold.

And yet it was as warm in the  as before.

Perhaps I'm ill, thought the , and wound

a  round his neck.

If only I had a , thought the

and buried itself deep into its  of  .

They were both so terribly unhappy.

Then a little  came to see them.

"Hello," it whimpered. "It's so cold outside.

Can I come in to warm up?"

"Of course," growled the  kindly.

"Of course," neighed the .

The little thanked them and made itself

comfortable.

"Have you known each other long?"

the little  asked.

and nodded.

"Where did you meet?"

"In a 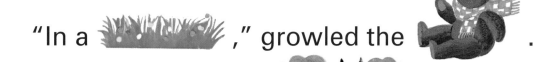," growled the .

"In the middle of a ," continued

the .

"Under an ," they both explained at

the same time.

"Then you're friends?" asked the  .

"Yes," growled the .

"That is true," agreed the  , for it was

the truth.

Anything else would be a lie.

"Why are you standing with your backs to each

other?" asked the little  .

Yes, why indeed?

And because they didn't want to admit that they had

quarrelled,  and  turned round again.

They lay down by the  with the  and

chatted.

And suddenly it was warm again.

The  took off his , and the

forgot the  .

When the winter was over, they said goodbye to the

little  and went back to the  in

the  and to the   .

One day, the  visited them.

 and saw that they had both been

wrong.

The of the  were .

All **3** of them laughed.

Sigrid Heuck:
Pony, Bear and Snowstorm
Aus dem Deutschen von Hilary Schmitt-Thomas
ISBN 3 522 43484 6

Gesamtausstattung: Sigrid Heuck
Schrift: Univers 55
Satz: Marlis Killermann in Winnenden
Reproduktion: Photolitho AG in Gossau/Zürich
Druck und Bindung: J. P. Himmer in Augsburg
© 2004 by Thienemann Verlag
(Thienemann Verlag GmbH), Stuttgart/Wien
Printed in Germany. Alle Rechte vorbehalten.
5 4 3 2 1* 04 05 06 07

Thienemann im Internet: www.thienemann.de

CE

A picture story about

a  and a !

THIENEMANN

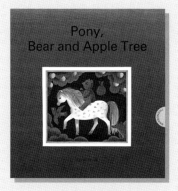

Pony,
Bear and Apple Tree

Sigrid Heuck
Pony, Bear and Apple Tree
32 Seiten
ISBN 3 522 43463 3

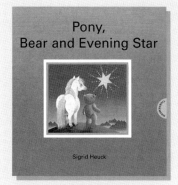

Pony,
Bear and Evening Star

Sigrid Heuck

Sigrid Heuck
Pony, Bear and Evening Star
32 Seiten
ISBN 3 522 43474 9

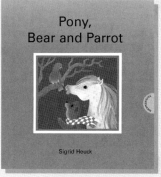

Pony,
Bear and Parrot

Sigrid Heuck

Sigrid Heuck
Pony, Bear and Parrot
32 Seiten
ISBN 3 522 43475 7

**Die Bilderbuchklassiker für Englisch-Anfänger.
In einfachen Sätzen, mit großer Schrift und vielen Bildern,
die das Verständnis erleichtern.**

- **einfache Sätze**
- **große Schrift**
- **Hauptwörter zum leichteren
Verständnis durch Bilder ersetzt**

third

fir twigs

mountains

bucket

cave

blanket

snow

sledge

lantern

ball

fire

bed

pot

owl